W9-AGD-015

Walt Disney

Lady
and the Tramp

Twin Books

One Christmas Eve many, many years ago, the streets and houses were covered with freshly fallen snow and lights burned brightly in every window. The air tingled with excitment. Soon it would be time to open the presents.

At last, the clock struck
midnight.

At Jim Dear and Darling's
home, many colorful boxes
lay under the Christmas
tree. "Here, open this one
first," said Jim Dear,
handing Darling a large
box.

"What is it?" asked
Darling.

"Open it and you'll see,"
said Jimmy Dear, smiling.

Darling had barely
undone the ribbon when out
jumped a cocker spaniel
puppy. "Oh, he is so cute!"
cried Darling.

"It's a she, and her name
is Lady," corrected Jim Dear.

6

Lady soon became the queen of the household. She was pampered and petted by everyone. And in return, she looked after the couple, fetching Jim Dear's newspaper and slippers and guarding the house at night.

For her birthday she received a beautiful blue collar. "Look at how pretty you are," said Darling. "Wait till the others see me," thought Lady.

Jock, the Scottish terrier, and Trusty, the bloodhound, were her neighbors. They were purebred dogs too, and very distinguished.

Trusty had once been a brilliant tracker. But he had grown old and his nose wasn't what it used to be.

"What a beautiful collar!" they exclaimed. "You've grown into a lovely little lady."

But although Lady enjoyed her pampered life, one day she noticed that things had slowly begun to change. No one seemed to pay much attention to her anymore. She didn't understand what was happening.

"What have I done wrong?" she asked herself. "This afternoon, Jim Dear rushed by without even giving me a pat on the head. And Darling spends all her time knitting. She hasn't taken me for a walk in ages. And what's all this talk about a 'happy event'?"

"A 'happy event,' Pigeon, is the worst thing that could happen to you."

Lady looked around in alarm. "Who is that dog?" she thought indignantly. "Look at that scruffy animal! He is not even wearing a collar! How dare he talk to me!"

"It's a cinch!" said the
stranger, whose name was
Tramp. "Your mistress is
going to have a baby! Some
brat will soon be pulling
your tail and jumping on
your back! Listen to me,
Pidge. Leave that fancy
collar behind and skedaddle
out of here!"

"So long and good luck!"
he added with a wink, and
was gone in a flash.

Tramp, the mongrel, was right. Within a few days the house was buzzing with activity. People came and went, bringing presents and making funny noises over a crib.

Lady was allowed to see the baby. "He's not so awful," she thought. "In fact, he's rather cute. Perhaps we'll be friends."

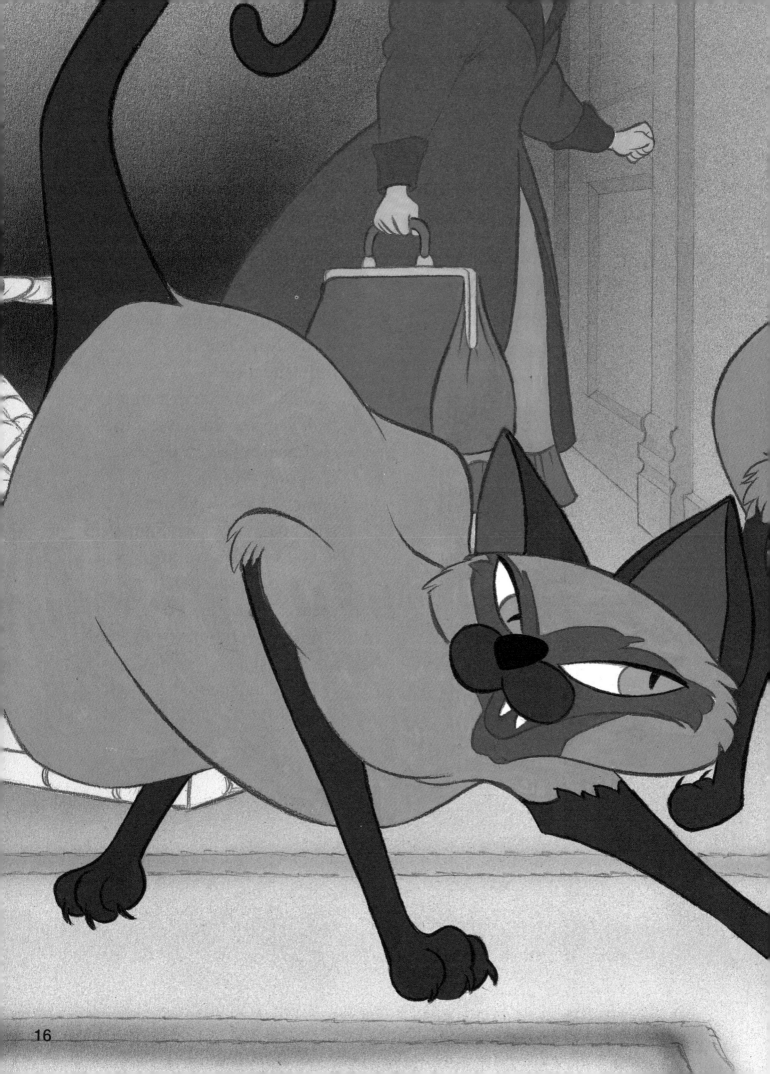

Soon everything was back to normal, but not for long. One day a fierce-looking woman with a suitcase came to the door.

"Lady, this is Aunt Sarah," said Darling. "She's going to look after the baby while Jim Dear and I take a little vacation."

With Aunt Sarah came two Siamese cats, who took over the house in no time.

Si and Am were their names. They were crafty and bold. "We are Siamese if you please! We are Siamese if you don't please!" they hissed. "Where we come from, cats are kings!"

The cats sneered at poor Lady.

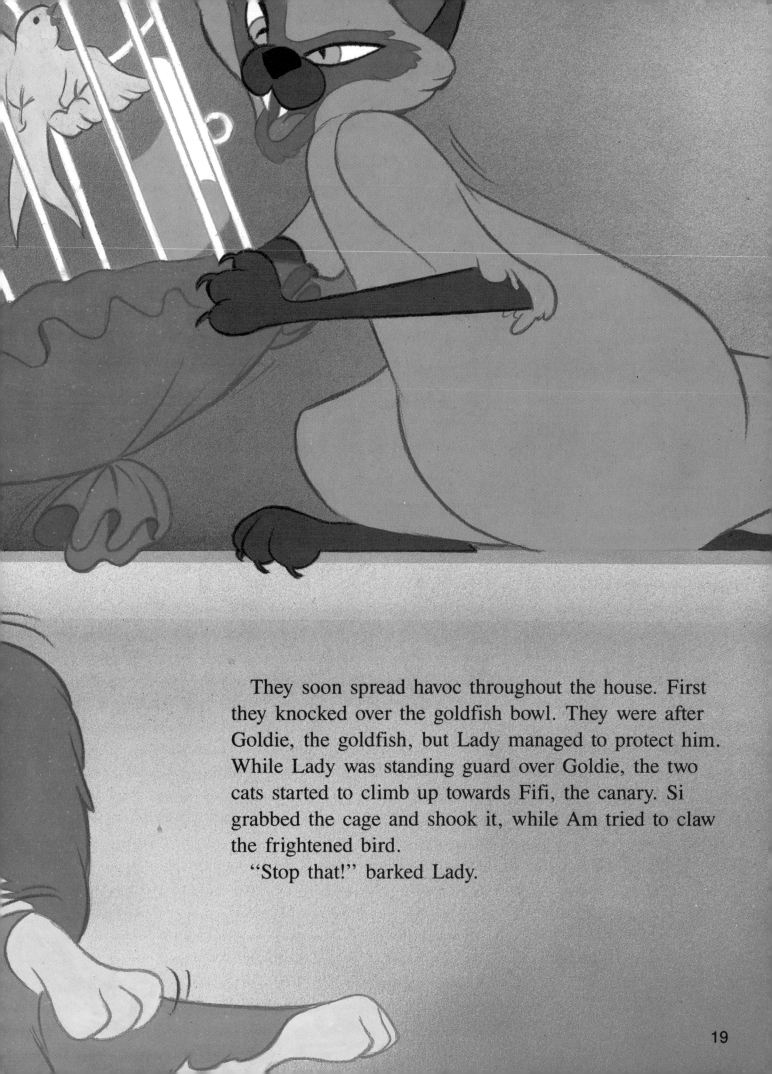

They soon spread havoc throughout the house. First they knocked over the goldfish bowl. They were after Goldie, the goldfish, but Lady managed to protect him. While Lady was standing guard over Goldie, the two cats started to climb up towards Fifi, the canary. Si grabbed the cage and shook it, while Am tried to claw the frightened bird.

"Stop that!" barked Lady.

Crash! Bang! The cage fell, knocking down a painting.

Aunt Sarah came rushing into the room. "What is this?" she demanded, pointing at the mess. Si and Am purred sweetly, pretending all innocence. Aunt Sarah glared at Lady. "You naughty dog! You'll be punished for this!" she threatened as she carried off the two cats. "My poor babies," she cooed into their ears. "You musn't play with that wicked dog."

21

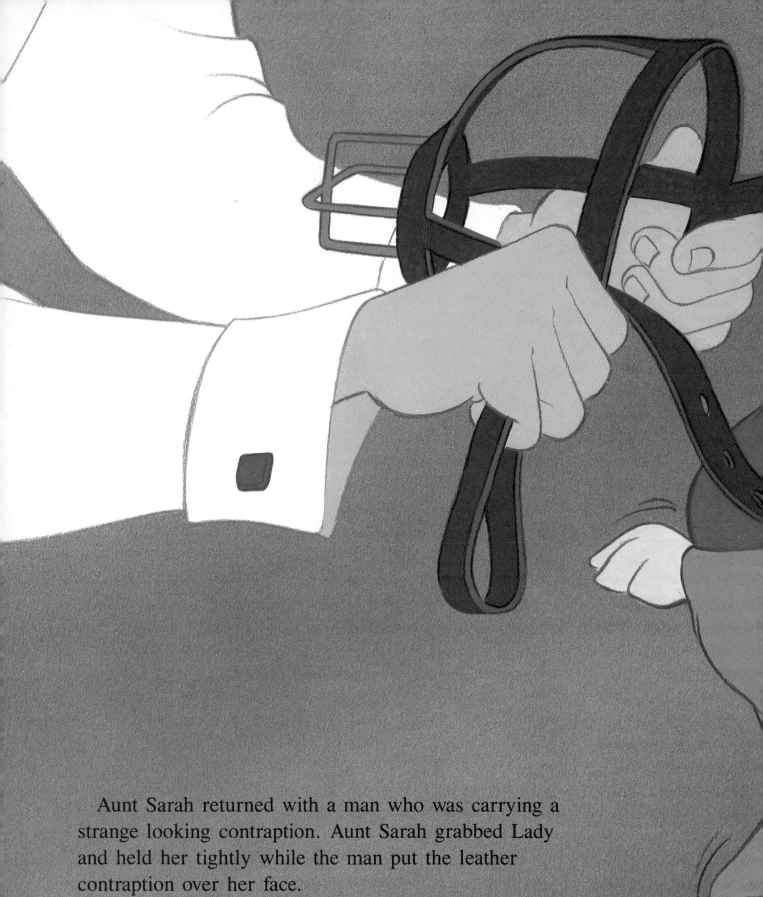

Aunt Sarah returned with a man who was carrying a strange looking contraption. Aunt Sarah grabbed Lady and held her tightly while the man put the leather contraption over her face.

"A muzzle!" cried Lady. "What are they doing to me? Oh! I wish that Jim Dear and Darling were here." She wriggled her way out of Aunt Sarah's arms and fled out of the house.

Poor Lady was so
frightened that she ran
without watching where she
was going.

She rushed in between
passing cars and along
crowded streets. She wanted
to get as far away from
Aunt Sarah as possible.

A gang of stray dogs, seeing her dash by, started to chase after her. Wearing a muzzle, she was easy game for them. When she heard the dogs behind her, Lady ran even faster.

Tramp, who was nearby, also heard the dogs, and turned just in time to see what was happening. "Poor little thing! I'd better go and help her!" he thought to himself as he took off after the dogs.

When Tramp caught up with the dogs he saw that Lady was cornered by two of the snarling animals.

"Aren't you guys ashamed of yourselves? Picking on a defenseless creature!" growled Tramp, leaping to Lady's rescue. "Scram, you two — before I make hamburger meat out of you!"

"It's Tramp!" yapped one of the bullies. "Let's get out of here!" They slunk off with their tails between their legs.

"Hi there, Pigeon! Tramp at your service. King of the mutts and Prince of the mongrels. Always ready for a scuffle." Tramp peered at Lady. "Hey, haven't I seen you before?" he asked, pricking up his ears.

Poor Lady couldn't speak — not with the muzzle over her face.

"I've got it!" shouted Tramp. "You're the one whose mistress was having a baby! What are you doing so far from home? And who put that muzzle on you?"

Tramp realized that Lady could not answer him because her jaws were held together by the muzzle. "Follow me, Pidge! We'll have that thing off you in a jiffy." Tramp led her to the Zoo.

They stopped at the crocodile's cage. "This should do it. Just stick your nose through these bars," suggested Tramp. But Lady didn't like the gleam in the crocodile's eyes. He looked more hungry than helpful.

When Tramp saw Lady back away in fear, he decided to look for another solution. They came across Busy Beaver, who was hard at work.

"Hi there, Busy! How about giving us a hand — or should I say a tooth?" chuckled Tramp.

Busy waddled up to Lady and looked her over. "Hmm. Let me see. Oh, this should be no problem. A few gnaws here and there and we'll have that muzzle off in no time!"

Busy knew his job well. His sharp teeth gnawed furiously at the muzzle, and with a loud snap, it came off.

"Oh, Mr. Beaver," said Lady. "I don't know how I can ever thank you!" She wagged her tail in gratitude.

"Think nothing of it. It was my pleasure," replied Busy Beaver with a gracious bow.

"And now I bet you're hungry, Pidge. Come on, I'll treat you to dinner. I hope you like Italian food," said Tramp as he guided Lady to the back of a little Italian restaurant.

"Trrammp! Watta gooda suprisa!" beamed Tony the chef. "And who is your *bella fidanzata?*"

"What's a *bella fidanzata?*" thought Lady.

Tony was a real romantic. Soon he had the two dogs eating a delicious spaghetti dinner by candlelight. And while they ate, he played his accordion and sang love songs. This was all very new to Lady. She was enjoying herself and told Tramp about the baby, the Siamese cats and Aunt Sarah.

After dinner, Tramp took Lady for a stroll in the park. There was a full moon. "He's really not so bad," thought Lady. "He's not a purebred like me, but there's something special about him."

The two dogs fell asleep under the stars. Each dreamed of the other.

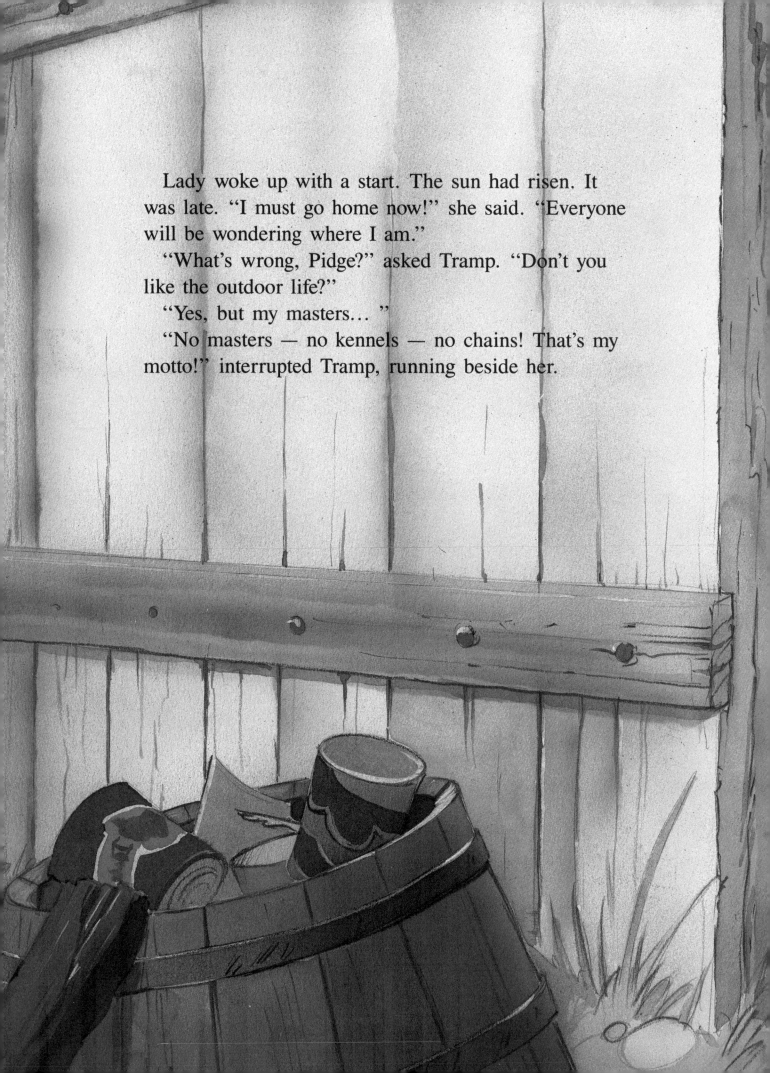

Lady woke up with a start. The sun had risen. It was late. "I must go home now!" she said. "Everyone will be wondering where I am."

"What's wrong, Pidge?" asked Tramp. "Don't you like the outdoor life?"

"Yes, but my masters... "

"No masters — no kennels — no chains! That's my motto!" interrupted Tramp, running beside her.

Tramp stopped suddenly. "Do you hear what I hear? Chickens! And chickens mean eggs, and eggs mean breakfast!" Before Lady could stop him, Tramp dived into the midst of the clucking hens.

"Stop! Don't do that!" cried Lady. "Someone will catch you!" But Tramp was having much too much fun.

Ping! Ping! Bullets flew about them.

"Run for it, Pidge. Someone is shooting at us,"
yelled Tramp.

"I knew he'd get caught," thought Lady. "And look
at him laughing. He thinks this is just a joke."

Tramp ran on ahead and disappeared around the
corner. "Wait for me, Tramp!" begged Lady.

Tramp was too far ahead to hear Lady's cries. When Lady stopped to catch her breath, a truck screeched to a halt. Two men jumped out and grabbed her. "This is the thief!" one of them said. "Caught redhanded. Look! There are feathers in her fur."

Before she knew what had happened, Lady found herself behind bars at the city dog pound. Never had she seen so many scruffy-looking dogs. Tears welled up in her eyes.

"Oh, dear! What did I get myself into?" she cried as the door slammed behind her.

"This ain't no deluxe hotel, that's for sure!" said Pedro the chihuahua.

"Where ya been all my life, honey?" teased the bulldog.

"Look at that collar — those gems ain't fakes. This dog's got money," said Boris the scrawny wolfhound.

"What'd you do? Give the maid fleas?" joked the others.

"Oh, come on now, fellas, leave the girl alone. Can't you see that the kid's got class?" said a sassy-looking female. "My name is Peg," she said to Lady. "What's yours?"

Lady introduced herself. "This Peg may not be a shrinking violet," she thought, "but she is certainly very kind."

"Don't worry, honey!" said Peg, winking. "Take it from someone who knows! A girl with your style won't stay here long."

55

Peg knew what she was talking about. Within a half hour, Lady was fetched by one of the guards and escorted home.

"So long, Duchess!" cried the dogs. "Don't forget us! Pound chains or house chains are all the same! Down with all chains!"

And speaking of chains, that's exactly what was waiting for Lady when she returned home. Aunt Sarah attached her to a doghouse with a short chain. She could barely move.

Jock and Trusty came to visit her. They felt sorry for their little friend. Lady was so ashamed she could barely speak.

Lady was sitting in the doghouse when she heard a familiar voice say, "Hi there, Pigeon! What's new?"

It was Tramp, acting as if nothing had happened.

Forgetting that she was chained, Lady ran up to him and nearly choked herself. "Ah! So now you come!" she said angrily. "Have you no shame? How dare you come here after all that you've done! Look at me! This is all your fault!" The fur on her back rose with anger.

"But Pidge..." began Tramp.

"And don't you call me 'Pidge' anymore!" she snarled.

"But... but... let me explain," stammered Tramp.

"There is nothing to explain. Go away! I don't ever want to see you again!" With that, Lady turned her back on him.

"What's with her?" wondered Tramp as he slouched away with his tail between his legs. "She thinks I am a good-for-nothing. How can I show her that I'm not so bad? She will never believe that I love her now."

That night, as Lady lay crying in the doghouse, a large rat crouched nearby, watching her. He was waiting for her to go to sleep so that he could slip into the warm house.

But Lady was too upset to sleep. She was feeling sad and lonely. She wished that Jim Dear and Darling would come back.

The rat was growing impatient. He decided to take a chance, and quietly sneaked toward the house.

The rat climbed up a tree next to the house and
jumped onto the roof. Lady saw him just as he was
slipping through the window to the baby's room.

"Woof! Woof!" she barked, running towards the
house. She'd forgotten about the chain again and almost
strangled herself once more.

Tramp, who had been sulking nearby, came running. "A rat!" cried Lady. "A big rat just went into the baby's room!"

"Don't worry, Pigeon! I'll get him for you!" shouted Tramp as he climbed into the house through a downstairs window.

Aunt Sarah had been awakened by Lady's barking. "What is that little pest up to now? If she keeps barking like that, she will wake up the baby!" Aunt Sarah was furious. "I am going to teach her a lesson!"

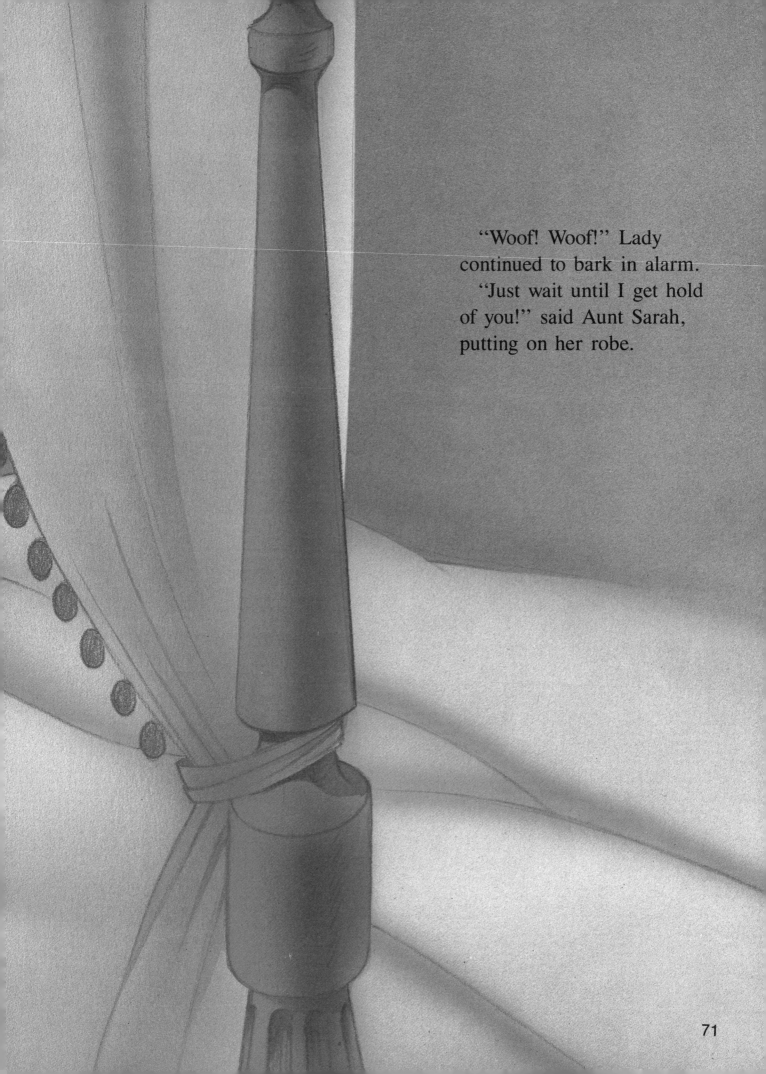

"Woof! Woof!" Lady
continued to bark in alarm.
"Just wait until I get hold
of you!" said Aunt Sarah,
putting on her robe.

Tramp finally reached the baby's room, and not a minute too soon! The rat was climbing up onto the baby's crib. Tramp jumped on top of him, growling ferociously. Startled, the rat lost its balance and fell to the floor. Tramp landed next to him and the two began to fight.

Fur flew and teeth flashed
as the two rolled around the
floor. But the rat was no
match for the angry Tramp.

Meanwhile Lady had
broken off her chain and ran
into the room. The rat lay
dead — Tramp had won the
fight!

Lady looked at Tramp, who was licking his wounds. He was a bit scratched, but that was all. The noise had wakened the baby, who began to cry. "Wah! Wah!" screamed the baby at the top of his lungs.

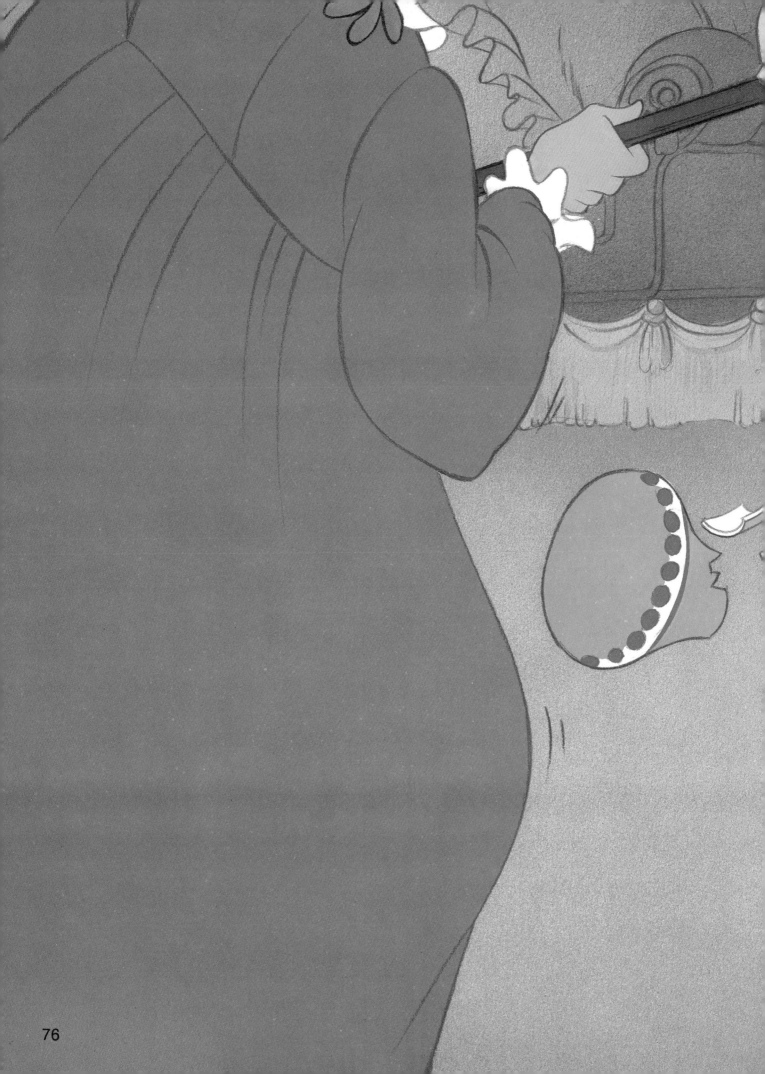

Lady was thanking Tramp when Aunt Sarah stormed
into the room. She was purple with rage and was
carrying a broom! She didn't notice the dead rat. She
only had eyes for the two dogs.

"Out of here, you two! Down to the cellar! It's the
dog pound for you — and this time it will be forever!"

A swish of the broom and the two unlucky dogs found themselves downstairs. The cellar door opened and they were thrust into the dark!

Suddenly, Lady heard familiar voices above. "It's Jim Dear and Darling! They've come home!" she told Tramp.

Within a few minutes the cellar door opened. "Lady!
Here, Lady! Come on, girl!" called Jim Dear. Lady
told Tramp to stay put and ran up the stairs into her
master's arms. At the same time, two men from the
dog pound arrived at the house. Aunt Sarah told them
about Tramp and they went to the cellar and grabbed
him. Tramp was rushed into a waiting van.

Trusty and Jock saw him as he was driven away.
"We must help the old fellow," said Jock. "He may not
be a purebred dog, but he is a good one!"

"Well, Lady! What's all this I hear about you misbehaving?" asked Jim Dear sternly.

Lady knew that she couldn't explain what had happened. She had to show them the dead rat. "They will understand if they see it," she thought. She ran towards the stairs hoping they would follow her.

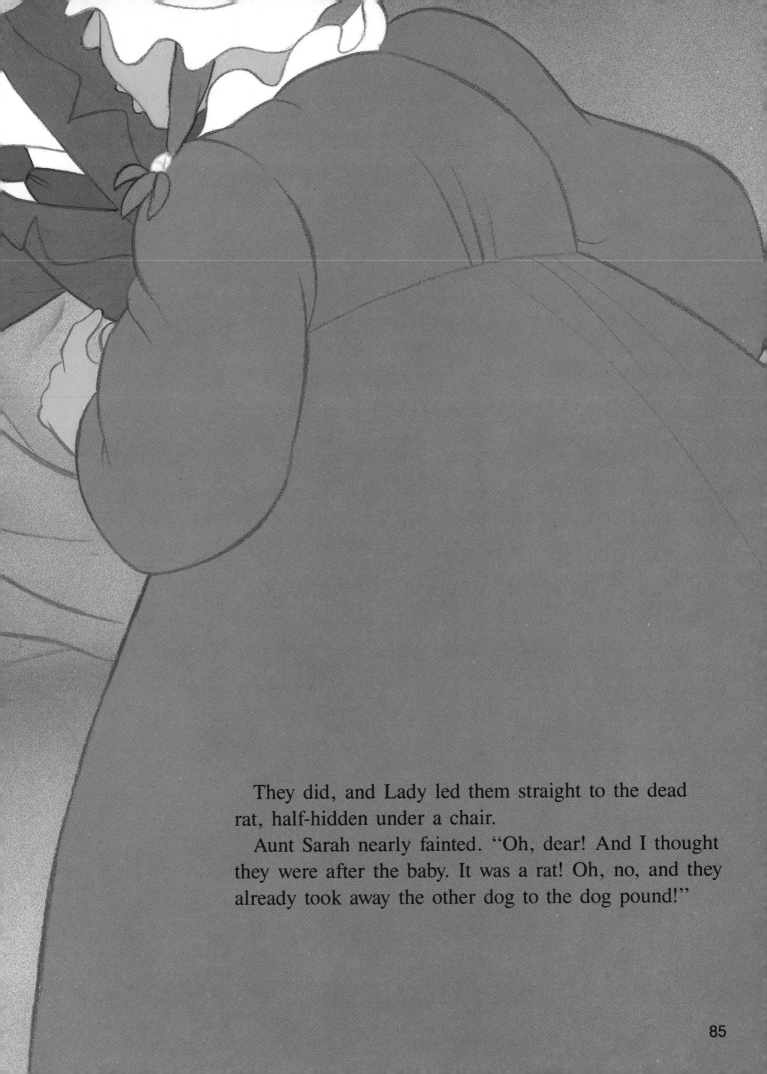

They did, and Lady led them straight to the dead rat, half-hidden under a chair.

Aunt Sarah nearly fainted. "Oh, dear! And I thought they were after the baby. It was a rat! Oh, no, and they already took away the other dog to the dog pound!"

"Come with me, Lady!" shouted Jim Dear. "We'll find your friend. He saved our baby's life! It's the very least we can do," he said as they left the house to find a cab.

In the cab, Lady began to worry that they might be too late. "Faster! Please hurry!" she called to the driver, and to Jim she explained, "He is no saint.... He is not really handsome either... but I love him all the same!"

In the meantime, Trusty and Jock had followed the dog pound carriage with the help of Trusty's nose. "I am not so old after all," said Trusty, and he was very proud.

"I'll head him off," he told Jock as he ran in front of the horse. The horse was frightened and reared up, knocking over the carriage.

Lady and Jim Dear finally caught up with the dog pound carriage. Jim Dear talked to the driver and Lady ran around to the back.

"Oh, Tramp! Are you hurt?" she asked him.

"Hi there, Pidge! I am just fine!" answered Tramp. Nothing could harm that old scoundrel.

"Tell me something, Tramp," said Lady several weeks later. "What does a *bella fidanzata* mean?"

Tramp looked at Lady and grinned. "You've got a good memory, Pidge! It means… ummm… a beautiful fiancee! And you are, aren't you?"

And so Lady and the Tramp became engaged and were soon married. Trusty, his leg in a bandage, but otherwise fine, and Jock, wearing his new plaid jacket, congratulated the happy couple.

"If it hadn't been for you, Trusty, I'd be dead. Thank you!" said Tramp.

"It was nothing, old man. All in a day's work!" replied the proud Trusty.

Christmas Eve came again. But this time there were one... two... three... four puppies under the tree!

Produced by
Twin Books
15 Sherwood Place,
Greenwich, CT 06830 USA

© 1986 The Walt Disney Company

All rights reserved. No part of this publication may be
reproduced or transmitted in any form by any means
without prior permission from the Publisher.

ISBN 1 85469 977 6

Reprinted in 1992

Printed in Italy

10 9 8 7 6 5 4 3 2 1